Rabbit-cadabra!

BUNNICULA
..and friends..

#4

Rabbit-cadabra!

by **James Howe**

illustrated by **Jeff Mack**

Ready-to-Read

Aladdin

New York   London   Toronto   Sydney

ALADDIN PAPERBACKS
An imprint of Simon & Schuster Children's Publishing Division
1230 Avenue of the Americas, New York, NY 10020
Text copyright © 1993, 2006 by James Howe
Illustrations copyright © 2006 by Jeff Mack
Text adapted by Heather Henson from *Rabbit-Cadabra!* by James Howe
All rights reserved, including the right of reproduction in whole or in part in any
form.
READY-TO-READ, ALADDIN PAPERBACKS, and related logo are registered
trademarks of Simon & Schuster, Inc.
Also available in an Atheneum hardcover edition.
Designed by Abelardo Martínez
The text of this book was set in Century Old Style.
The illustrations for this book were rendered in acrylic.
Manufactured in the United States of America
First Aladdin Paperbacks edition August 2007
10 9 8 7 6 5 4 3 2 1
The Library of Congress has cataloged the hardcover edition as follows:
Howe, James, 1946–
Rabbit-cadabra! / James Howe ; illustrated by Jeff Mack.—1st ed.
p. cm.—(Bunnicula and friends ; #4)
Summary: When Chester learns that the Amazing Karlovsky will use a rabbit in
his school magic show, he comes up with a plan to stop vampire bunnies.
ISBN-13: 978-0-689-85727-0 (hc.)
ISBN-10: 0-689-85727-6 (hc.)
[1. Magicians—Fiction. 2. Cats—Fiction. 3. Dogs—Fiction. 4. Rabbits—Fiction.]
I. Mack, Jeff, ill. II. Title. III. Series.
PZ7.H83727Rab 2006
[Fic]—dc22
2004026321
ISBN-13: 978-0-689-85752-2 (pbk.)
ISBN-10: 0-689-85752-7 (pbk.)

To the Amazing Kristy Raffensberger
—J. H.

For my brother, Brian
—J. M.

CHAPTER 1:

The Magician

One day when Toby came home from school, he woke me up from my nap. He was so excited he could hardly stand still.

In fact, he was jumping up and down.

"Harold, guess what?" Toby asked.

I perked up my ears to let Toby know that I really, really wanted to guess what.

I live with the Monroes, and I like them all a lot, but Toby is my favorite. He's good about explaining things, and he's good about sharing his snacks.

"The Amazing Karlovsky is coming to town!" Toby said. "I can't wait!"

I wagged my tail and woofed to show that I couldn't wait either, even though I had no idea what Toby was talking about.

Who was the Amazing Karlovsky, and why was he coming to town?

That night I asked Chester about
it. Chester reads a lot of books. If
this Karlovsky was so amazing, I
thought there might be a book about
him.

"The Amazing Karlovsky
is a magician," Chester said.

"A magician? What's that?"
asked Howie. He's still a puppy,
and so he asks a lot of questions.

"Magicians do tricks, like pulling
rabbits out of hats," Chester
explained.

"Why?" Howie wanted to know, and
I must admit I was curious, too.

"Beats me." Chester shrugged. "Anyway, I don't know why Toby is so excited about this Amazing Karlovsky when the real magician around here is the rabbit."

We all turned to look at Bunnicula. He was sitting in his cage, sleeping. That's what he does all day. Sleep. He wakes up after dark.

"Can Bunnicula pull *himself* out of a hat?" Howie asked.

Chester sighed. "No, Howie. But he can get out of his cage before you can say hocus-pocus. And he turns vegetables white."

"He looks pretty harmless now," Howie said.

"Don't be fooled!" Chester replied. "Bunnicula is not only a magician, he is a vampire!"

"Is that really true?" Howie asked. He is the newest member of our household, so he wasn't around when the Monroes first brought Bunnicula home.

"Of course it's true!" Chester said.

I didn't say anything. I had learned a long time ago not to argue with Chester.

It is true that strange things happen from time to time around our house. Vegetables *do* turn white. But it is also true that Chester can get a little carried away.

CHAPTER 2:

Signs

The next morning Chester, Howie, and I went for our morning walk. We'd gone only a few blocks when Chester stopped in his tracks.

"What is it?" I asked.

"Look!" Chester cried. "There!"

Tacked to a telephone pole was a poster that read:

"The Amazing Karlovsky!"

The picture showed a guy in a top hat holding a rabbit. But it wasn't just any rabbit. It had white fur with black patches like a cape. The eyes seemed to glow red. Two tiny fangs seemed

to glisten where little bunny teeth
should have been.

"It's Bunnicula!" I said. "But how
could it be?"

"I don't know," Chester said.
"But I'm going to find out."

Later that afternoon Chester
woke me from a perfectly good nap.

With all the excitement around here, I was beginning to wonder if I'd ever finish a nap again.

"I've got it all figured out!" he announced. "I don't think it was Bunnicula on that poster after all."

"It looked like Bunnicula," said Howie.

"I know," Chester replied, "but I think it's a cousin from the old country."

"The old country?" Howie asked.

"Transylvania," Chester answered. "That's where Bunnicula came from."

"It's where Chester *thinks* Bunnicula came from," I corrected.

"I thought he came from a movie theater," Howie said.

"That's where the Monroes found him, but he comes from Transylvania," Chester replied. "I think this Karlovsky must come from Transylvania, too."

"So?" I had no idea where Chester was going with this. I wasn't sure I wanted to know.

"So we all know what else comes from Transylvania, don't we?" Chester asked.

"Coffee beans?" Howie piped up.

"Vampires!" Chester shouted.

Howie gasped. I rolled my eyes.

"Follow me," said Chester.

I thought Chester was being silly, but I followed him anyway. When we reached Toby and Pete's school, Chester pointed to a sign.

"See!?"

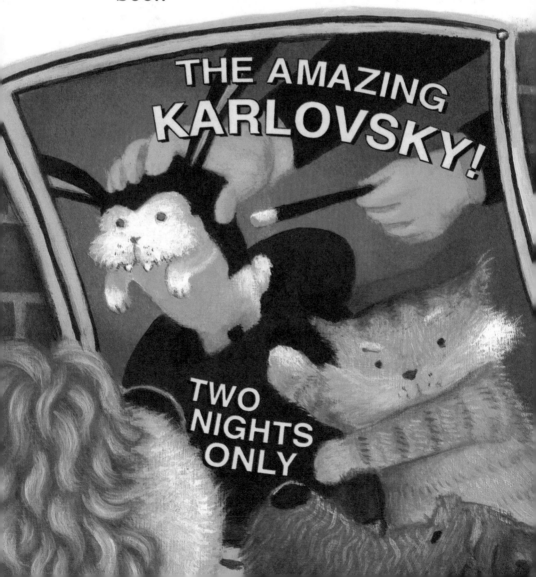

THE AMAZING KARLOVSKY!

TWO NIGHTS ONLY

"I see why Toby was so excited," I replied. "The Amazing Karlovsky is performing tonight."

"Don't you get it, Harold?" Chester cried. "The Amazing Karlovsky is a magician from Transylvania who pulls rabbits out of his hat! But what kind of rabbits?"

"Transylvanian rabbits?" Howie guessed.

"Vampire rabbits!" Chester cried. "This Karlovsky character is pulling vampire rabbits out of a hat. Think of it! If he really *is* a magician, there could be hundreds of vampire rabbits by now. We've got to stop him before it's too late!"

CHAPTER 3:

The Plan

Chester kept to himself for the rest of the day.

I guess he was coming up with a plan. I was not looking forward to Chester's plan. Chester's plans usually mean trouble.

After supper the Monroes got ready to go to the show.

"How do I look?" Toby shouted as he rushed into the room.

He was wearing a long black cape and a black top hat. He waved a magic wand in the air.

I woofed to let Toby know I thought
he looked great, but Pete laughed
at him.

"You're only going to be in
the audience!" he said.

"Maybe the Amazing Karlovsky
will call me up on stage to be his
assistant!" Toby replied.

"Fat chance," said Pete.

As soon as the Monroes were gone, Chester appeared.

"Okay," he said. "The coast is clear. First, we need some garlic."

"Not garlic again," I sighed. "Don't you remember what happened the last time you got into the garlic?"

"Did you do some cooking?" Howie asked.

"Not exactly," I said. I was about to tell Howie all about it, but Chester cut me off.

"Garlic stops vampires," he said and marched into the kitchen. He went through all the cabinets.

"No garlic!" he cried. "How can this be?"

"What about cinnamon?" Howie asked. "Or chili powder?"

Chester glared at Howie, then his eyes lit up. "I know where we can find some garlic."

"Where?" I asked, although I didn't really want to know.

Without a word, Chester dashed out the pet door. Howie and I had no choice but to follow.

I couldn't believe where Chester took us.

It was the alley behind Mr. Pizza. The Dumpster was full of old half-eaten pizzas.

"How lucky!" said Chester.

"Lucky?!" I yelped, holding a paw over my nose. "Yucky is more like it."

Chester didn't seem to notice the smell. He had a gleam in his eye. That gleam always makes me nervous.

"There's enough garlic on this pizza to wipe out an army of vampire bunnies!" Chester announced.

"If the smell doesn't wipe *us* out first," I muttered.

"Maybe we should take the pepperoni instead," Howie suggested. Howie really likes pepperoni.

Chester shook his head. "It's a well-known fact that pepperoni has no effect on vampires at all."

Howie looked at Chester with awe. I didn't have the heart to tell him that what Chester doesn't know, he makes up.

CHAPTER 4:

The Performance

When we got to the school, the parking lot was full.

"How are we going to get in without being seen?" Howie asked.

"Or smelled," I added.

"Quiet!" Chester ordered. "Follow me!"

We slipped through an open door and crept down a dark hallway.

In the distance we could hear the sound of clapping.

"Ladies and gentlemen!" a voice boomed. "Now for my final trick of the evening!"

"This is it!" Chester whispered. "Let's hurry!"

We turned a corner and ducked behind a curtain.

On the other side of the curtain, the Amazing Karlovsky was holding a top hat and a magic wand.

"Pulling a rabbit out of a hat sounds easy," the Amazing Karlovsky was saying, "but a magician needs just the right hat—and just the right rabbit!"

"Right rabbit, indeed," Chester muttered, then he turned to me. "All right, Harold, here's what I want you to do."

He explained the plan.

"Why me?" I said, but I didn't have time to say anything else.

The Amazing Karlovsky was waving a bunch of carrots in the air.

"To make our rabbit appear, first we must get his attention," the magician's voice boomed. "And what do rabbits love most?"

"CARROTS!" the audience shouted. Slowly the Amazing Karlovsky lowered the carrots into the hat. Then he waved his magic wand.

"Rabbit-cadabra!" he bellowed. "Appear!"

"Now!" Chester yelled and shoved me onto the stage with the pizza clamped between my teeth.

The Amazing Karlovsky was amazed. The audience went wild.

"Don't just stand there!" Chester hissed. "Get the hat!"

I raced across the stage, tossed
the pizza in the air, and grabbed
the hat.

A rabbit jumped out. He was holding
a bunch of carrots in his mouth.
White carrots!

The audience cheered.
The Amazing Karlovsky slipped
on the pizza.

Somebody grabbed the rabbit.
Somebody grabbed me. It was
Mrs. Monroe.

"Harold!" she cried. "What do you
think you're doing?"

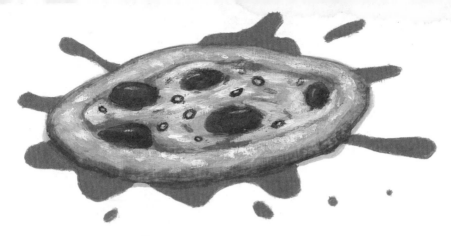

CHAPTER 5:

Mystery Solved—Or Not?

After the show we stood backstage with the Monroes and the Amazing Karlovsky.

"I'm sorry about what happened, Cousin Charlie," Mrs. Monroe said. "I know you were looking forward to performing this trick for the first time."

"Cousin Charlie?" Chester whispered.

"Yes, I've always wanted to make a rabbit appear out of a hat," said the Amazing Karlovsky. He laughed.

"I just didn't expect to make a pizza-delivery dog appear at the same time."

"I don't know what gets into our animals," Mr. Monroe said. "They act so strange sometimes."

"Cousin Charlie," Toby said. "I wish I could be a magician like you."

"Maybe one day you will be," said the Amazing Karlovsky. "Meanwhile, would you like to be my assistant at tomorrow night's show?"

"Wow!" said Toby, glancing at Pete. "Would I ever!"

Later that night after the Monroes had gone to bed, Chester, Howie, and I sat in the living room.

"Well, Chester. What do you think of all your ideas now?" I asked.

Chester did not answer. He was watching Bunnicula.

"The Amazing Karlovsky is not from Transylvania, after all," I continued. "He is just plain old Cousin Charlie."

"Why does he call himself
the Amazing Karlovsky?"
Howie asked.

"I guess the Amazing Charlie
doesn't sound very mysterious,"
I answered.

"But how did Bunnicula get
in that poster?" Howie wanted
to know.

"Cousin Charlie must have
used our bunny for his publicity
photo," I replied.

We were all quiet for a moment,
and then Chester finally spoke up.

"So, Harold."

"Yes, Chester?"

"Would you like to explain
how the carrots turned white?"

Howie gulped.

I turned to look at Bunnicula,
and—I couldn't help it—a chill
ran through me. The little bunny
was smiling.

We did not get to see the Amazing Karlovsky's second show. We heard that he pulled Bunnicula out of his hat without a hitch—and without a pizza.

Toby learned how the trick was done, but of course he isn't telling anyone.

Even Toby doesn't know how those carrots turned white, however. The Amazing Karlovsky himself says he's never seen anything like it.

But then—that was no ordinary rabbit he pulled out of his hat, was it?